THE
RUPERT
ANNUAL

EXPRESS NEWSPAPERS

EGMONT
We bring stories to life

Published in Great Britain 2014 by Egmont UK Limited
The Yellow Building, 1 Nicholas Road, London W11 4AN
Rupert Bear™ & © 2014 Classic Media Distribution Limited/Express Newspapers.
All Rights Reserved.

ISBN 978 1 4052 7208 7
57515/1
Printed in Italy

No. 79

RUPERT and

RUPERT CALLS ON PODGY PIG

*"What's Podgy doing kneeling there?
Is something wrong?" thinks Rupert Bear.*

*"My gate is splintered, as you see,
What's more, it was done purposely!"*

One day Rupert starts bright and early in search of his chums. He calls first on Podgy Pig, and is surprised to find him gazing intently at his gate, which is badly splintered. "I say!" breathes Rupert. "Something jolly heavy must have struck this!" His chum sighs deeply. "It must have happened during the night," he says. "Did you hear any noises while you were in bed, Rupert?" "Why, no," says the little bear. "I went off to sleep straightaway. I didn't wake up until Mummy called me this morning." "Well, I heard something," says Podgy darkly. "I can't tell you what the time was, but some crashes and bangs woke me up—just when I was dreaming I had a picnic all to myself. I thought it was a thunderstorm, but I wonder if it could have been old Grimblegruff." "Who?" gasps Rupert, looking startled. "I don't know anyone of that name."

This book belongs to

....

CONTENTS

Edited by Stephanie Milton. *Designed by* Martin Aggett.
Cover illustrated by Stuart Trotter.

Endpapers illustrated by John Harrold.

he BOFFIT

RUPERT PROMISES TO LOOK

*"That window's in a dreadful state!
Whoever smashed it broke the gate."*

*"Has any other harm been done?"
And Rupert sets off at a run.*

"I don't suppose you do," grunts Podgy. "I read a book about him before I went to bed. He's a huge giant who goes around knocking down houses and things. He *could* have come here, you know." Rupert laughs at Podgy's solemn face. "But that only happened in a *book*," he says. "It isn't true—he's just a story giant!" "I expect you're right," mutters Podgy. "Anyway, just look at this!" He marches up the path and points to a broken window. "Whoever damaged the gate smashed that window as well!" he says. "I wish I knew who did it!" Rupert is as baffled as his chum, but suddenly the little bear has an idea. "Perhaps someone else has had something damaged," he suggests. "Suppose I could scout round and see." Podgy eagerly agrees, and saying goodbye, Rupert races away. "It didn't *look* like an accident. But who would damage Podgy's cottage?" he says.

RUPERT SEES MORE DAMAGE

Now he hears talk, to left and right,
Of houses damaged in the night.

"Gaffer is worried, I can tell,
Has he found something wrong as well?"

When Rupert tells his story through,
He's told, "This fence is damaged too!"

A smashed milk-bottle Rupert spies,
"There's trouble everywhere!" he cries.

As he runs along, Rupert keeps a sharp lookout, but he reaches the village without seeing anything unusual. Then outside one of the shops he overhears Mrs Badger and her friends talking about the damage done to their houses during the night. "So Podgy wasn't the only one," murmurs Rupert. Glancing ahead, he spies Gaffer Jarge peering at his fence in a puzzled way. "Hello, something else is wrong," mutters Rupert, and he hurries forward. Rupert finds the Gaffer prodding angrily at a broken paling. "You too!" Rupert gasps. "Everyone I've met seems to have had something damaged!" "If that be so," wheezes the old man, "then there's mischief afoot, and no mistake!" He shakes his head on hearing Rupert's story, then turns back to his splintered fence. Saying goodbye, Rupert hurries on, until suddenly he notices a shattered milk-bottle. "More trouble!" he whispers. "I don't understand this at all! Perhaps the Gaffer was right."

RUPERT PAUSES ON HIS WAY

"Who's done all this?" Then off he goes
To see if the Professor knows.

Gasps Rupert, "Here's a mystery!
There's sticking-plaster on this tree!"

An Imp of Spring pops into sight,
"A lot of trees got bruised last night."

"A frightful thing came bumping past,
It whirled into our home at last!"

By now Rupert is wondering what he will discover next. "I'll call and see if the Professor has any news," he decides. "Maybe there's been some damage at his castle too." All at once he stops short, unable to believe his eyes. Just ahead he can see a tree with large pieces of sticking-plaster on its trunk! The little bear runs to examine it. "Of all the odd things!" he gasps. "Whatever can it mean?" Suddenly, to Rupert's astonishment, an Imp of Spring wearing a first-aid armlet pops round the tree. "Excuse me," the Imp sighs, setting down a box of sticking-plaster. "I've lots more trees to patch. They got bruised last night, so I'm busy ... " "Last night!" interrupts Rupert excitedly. "D'you know who did it?" "It wasn't a person, but a strange thing," frowns the Imp. "And now it's in one of our underground passages!" He points out a secret entrance behind some roots. The little bear pauses uncertainly. "Dare I go in?" he wonders.

RUPERT GOES BELOW GROUND

"What is that noise like hammering?"
Then Rupert sees a fearsome thing.

It strikes the passage walls, bang—crash!
And hurtles past him, in a flash.

Then swerving back, it hits the ground,
Springs up with force, and whirls around.

He makes a grab, but all in vain,
Zig-zag! It thuds away again.

Rupert doesn't hesitate for long. Watched by the anxious Imp, he creeps gingerly down the steps. "What is that hammering noise?" he mutters, pausing at the bottom. Plucking up his courage, he moves cautiously along the gloomy passage. Next moment the hammering sound grows louder, and something comes hurtling towards him, striking the walls and shooting past him. Rupert sees that it is an object made of springs and buffers. "Whatever is it?" he gasps, too startled to move.

"I've never seen anything like it!" Before Rupert can recover himself, the object comes swerving back, hits the ground at his heels, and whirls around. "I mustn't let it get away!" he gasps, springing after it. "But I wish I had someone to help me." He makes a wild grab as the thing bounces swiftly off the floor, but in a flash it is out of his reach, thudding and zig-zagging its way along the passage. "It's escaped!" gasps the little bear. "It's too fast for me!"

10

RUPERT WATCHES IN ALARM

The little bear gives chase once more,
And sees it vanish through a door.

While frightened Imps crouch in their beds,
That thing swirls madly round their heads.

It strikes the floor at one Imp's heels,
"Get that thing out of here!" he squeals.

"Quick, catch it! Catch it, little bear!
It simply must not go down there!"

Rupert sets off in chase and soon he reaches some stone steps. "There it is!" he gasps. Narrowly missing a lamp, the object shoots through an open door, and as it vanishes Rupert hears squeals of alarm from the other side. "Someone's in there!" he cries, racing up the steps. He peeps nervously through the doorway and finds that the object has roused some of the Imps from their sleep. It is spinning and bumping about between their beds. "What's happening?" cries one of the Imps. The little bear creeps into the room, but he can only stare helplessly at the object, while the Imps try to keep out of its way, dodging this way and that. "Take it out!" shouts one. "Stop the thing!" squeals another. Nobody asks why Rupert is there, and the little bear hardly knows what he is doing himself. Suddenly the object shoots past him into another passage, and he dashes after it, followed by a desperate Imp. "Catch it!" yells the Imp. "It mustn't go down there at any cost!"

RUPERT SEIZES HIS CHANCE

"It nearly hit me!" Rupert gasps.
His hands above his head he clasps.

Towards more Imps the object whirls,
Around their special flasks it twirls.

"Oh, catch it, please! It took us hours
To make that tonic for the flowers!"

"Now I can slam the lid down quick!"
Breathes Rupert. "This should do the trick."

"It's all very well asking me to catch it!" thinks Rupert. He ducks and covers his ears as the thing bounces back and hits the ceiling with a heavy thud. Following it round another bend, Rupert stares in dismay, for a group of Imps are working by some important-looking bottles. They cry out anxiously as the object hurtles past, and one Imp stops in the act of pulling a lever, "Help!" he cries as he spies Rupert. "Catch that thing! Quickly, quickly, before it breaks these bottles!"

Rupert runs after the twirling, twisting object until he feels quite dizzy. "Hurry! Hurry!" wails the Imp at the lever, covering his face with his hands as the thing swerves towards an open tank of freshly made flower tonic! Rupert tries desperately to stop it, but misses. Then he catches sight of the tank lid and swiftly stoops to pick it up. Next moment the object plunges into the precious mixture, spraying it in all directions. "Now's my chance!" breathes Rupert, rushing forward with the lid.

Rupert and the Boffit

RUPERT THROWS THE NETTING

The little bear does not succeed,
That object twists away at speed.

But Rupert is not beaten yet,
He cries, "Let's catch it in this net!"

"Take hold!" He spreads the net out wide,
And hopes to snare that thing inside.

"Got it!" That object, strange of shape,
Is captured, only to escape!

Rupert slams the lid down on to the tank, then looks up, only to see the object whirling away again! "You'll never catch it," says one of the Imps. "It's like a slippery fish!" "Fish!" echoes Rupert. "That's given me an idea. If only I had a net." The Imps hurriedly search their store-box and to Rupert's delight they find a large piece of netting. "This isn't going to be easy," says the little bear, as they help him spread it out. "But it might do the trick." Rupert takes the middle of the net himself and asks the Imps to hold up the edges as best they can. "This is the strangest fish I've ever tried to catch!" he says, as they move slowly forward. Suddenly the object comes hurtling noisily towards them and, quick as a flash, Rupert flings the net over it. "We've got it!" he cries, as the thing bounces fiercely about inside. Then they are all thrown backwards as the net tears and their catch breaks free. "It was a good idea," pants an Imp. "But it didn't work!"

RUPERT CRAWLS FROM A HOLE

"It's off again!" Up Rupert jumps,
He trails that strange thing by its bumps.

It mounts some steps and does not stop,
"Oh good, there's daylight at the top!"

Those steps lead out into the wood,
"The thing has disappeared! That's good!"

"These trees are thickly padded, yes!
But why, I simply cannot guess."

Feeling very shaky, Rupert picks himself up and helps the Imps to their feet. "Oh dear, that thing is stronger than I thought," he says. Leaving the Imps, he sets off in chase again. Guided by heavy thuds, he races down another passage and sees the object hurtle round a sharp bend. He follows it to the foot of some steps. "There's daylight at the top," he pants. "I do hope it goes straight out and doesn't bother the Imps any more. It's done enough damage already!" To Rupert's relief the weird object shoots straight through the opening at the top of the steps. He waits for a few moments, then, as nothing happens, he makes his way up and finds himself peeping from a hollow tree in the wood. "The thing has disappeared," he mutters, gazing round. "That's good! But—how very odd! All the trees are thickly padded." Rupert scrambles out on to the grass and prods one of the pads. "It's soft—like rubber," he murmurs. "My, what a lot of strange things I've seen today!"

RUPERT TELLS OF HIS CHASE

A man is crossing to a shed,
He wears a bandage round his head.

"Out of control, a boffit veered,
It bumped my head, then disappeared."

"You see, I build these fairground cars,
Their boffits cause the bumps and jars!"

"You think you've seen it? That's good news!
Then help me, there's no time to lose!"

Feeling very puzzled, Rupert wanders along until he comes to a house he has never seen before. At that moment a strange, inventor-like man comes out, wearing a bandage round his head. Rupert hesitates, then goes forward. "Is something wrong?" Rupert asks anxiously. "Are you hurt?" "No, it's only a bruise," says the stranger. "A boffit got out of control. It bumped my head, then bounced off out of sight. You've not seen it, I suppose." Before Rupert can reply, the stranger points to a small, shiny car. "I design bumper cars for fairgrounds," he explains. "The boffit's the part that makes them bump. It has powerful springs that ... " "I think I *have* seen it!" interrupts the little bear. And he tells his story. "H'm. I'll have to pay for the damage," says the man, as he pushes the little car on to the track. His next words take Rupert's breath away. "Hah, you're small enough to drive this!" he says. "Will you help me to capture the boffit?"

RUPERT TRIES THE MAN'S CAR

"Just use the bonnet like a trap.
And catch that missing boffit—snap!"

The little bear learns all he's shown,
Then bravely drives off, on his own.

A worried Imp stands by the lane,
He cries, "There goes that thing again!"

Across the hummocks Rupert sweeps,
While out of sight that boffit leaps.

Rupert feels rather uneasy as he thinks of the fierce boffit. Then he looks longingly at the little car. "Yes, I'll help you!" he tells the man. He clambers into the driving seat and the inventor shows him the controls and how to work a lever which will open the bonnet ready to trap the boffit. "I think I've got it all clear," says Rupert at last. He starts the car and finds himself gliding smoothly away. "Oo, this is exciting!" he laughs. "But I'm not looking forward to meeting the boffit again!"

As Rupert steers his way carefully through a glade he notices a worried Imp. "I've seen that horrid jumping thing again!" cries the Imp. "Look, there it is!" he adds excitedly as something hurtles past them. Rupert puts on speed and goes off in chase. The boffit seems to be everywhere at once. Then suddenly it leaps over a hedge and disappears. "Whew!" gasps the little bear. "I mustn't lose track of it now!" And swerving aside he drives over the hummocks.

RUPERT PULLS UP BY A TREE

Now Rupert pauses in his search,
"Those branches! How they heave and lurch!"

He gazes upwards with a frown,
As twigs and leaves come tumbling down.

"A horrid thing's disturbing us!"
A small bird cheeps. "It's dangerous!"

"The boffit!" Rupert starts to climb,
"How odd I didn't guess first time!"

By the time Rupert pulls up beyond the hedge, the boffit is nowhere to be seen. While he is wondering where it can be, something else makes him gasp. "That tree!" he says. "Golly, how its branches are jerking! The birds don't know what to do." Scrambling out of the car, Rupert peers up into the greenery. "My!" he exclaims, as twigs shower all around him. "Someone must be shaking those branches! What a shame, frightening the birds like that!" The little bear takes a step nearer.

"Please, is anyone up there?" he calls nervously. While Rupert is waiting for an answer a bird alights on a nearby twig. "Please help us!" it cheeps. "A great big thing has got into our tree. It won't keep still—and it won't go away!" "The boffit—that's what it is!" exclaims Rupert. "Why didn't I think of that before?" Swiftly he starts to climb the tree. The trunk has plenty of footholds, but the branches are jerking madly. "Oo-oh!" he gasps. "I hope I can keep my balance."

RUPERT SHAKES THE BRANCHES

He whispers, "I can see it now,
Wedged on that wildly jerking bough!"

"Just out of reach! I'll have to sit
On this big branch to get at it."

He sits, as though upon a horse,
Then shakes the bough with all his force.

The boffit springs free. "There you are!
Now I can catch it with the car."

Rupert gazes anxiously upwards. "It's best to climb near the middle," he decides. Then, taking great care, he goes slowly higher. Suddenly, he glimpses the boffit wedged on the end of a branch which is still jerking about. "It looks dangerous up there," mutters the little bear. "I can't possibly get on to that!" Instead, Rupert scrambles along a lower branch. It sways under his weight, but at last he finds himself below the boffit. "Now to catch it!" he pants, stretching up. But the boffit is just out of reach. For a moment Rupert stares at the thing as it jerks wildly above his head. "If only I could *knock* it down," he thinks desperately. "Then I could catch it with the car. Perhaps I can just reach it from here." Fixing himself firmly on his own branch, he manages to grip the branch above. He shakes it as hard as he is able, and suddenly the boffit springs free. It plunges to the ground, while the startled birds flutter round and chirp their thanks to Rupert.

RUPERT DRIVES AT TOP SPEED

"We want to thank you!" chirp the birds,
"We think you're just too brave for words!"

"The boffit!" Rupert dashes back,
He simply must keep on its track!

He gains upon it, sure and swift,
And makes that special bonnet lift.

The lever shudders in his hands,
As with a jolt that wild thing lands.

Making his way down the tree as quickly as possible, Rupert swings himself from the lowest branch and lands with a bump at the bottom. The flutter of wings makes him glance up to see the birds circling joyfully around. "We want to thank you!" chirps their leader. "You are a very brave little bear." Rupert bids the birds a hasty farewell, then dashes for his car just as the boffit hurtles past. "There it goes!" he pants, flinging himself into the driving-seat. "I must keep up with it this time!" The little car shoots forward down a slope. As it gathers speed, Rupert spies the bouncing boffit only a few feet away. "I wonder if I can catch it!" he gasps, quickly pulling the special lever. Up comes the bonnet, and at the same instant the boffit strikes a rock, then springs off again—straight into the front of the car. The lever shudders violently, but Rupert dare not slacken his grip. "I've just got to trap the boffit now," he tells himself. "I might not get another chance."

RUPERT HAS A BUMPY RIDE

He pushes back the lever—slam!
"I've trapped it! Oh, how glad I am!"

The car shoots forward, jumps and shakes,
Straight for the nearest tree it makes!

"I'll crash! The steering-wheel won't work!"
BOOMPS! Up he goes, with such a jerk!

Rocketing onward crazily,
He cannons into every tree.

Although he feels slightly dazed by the jolting of the boffit Rupert remembers exactly what he must do. He pushes back the lever and slams down the car bonnet. "I've trapped it!" he sighs in relief. "I've caught the ... oo-oo!" Rupert breaks off in alarm as the boffit suddenly seems to go wild. The car shoots forward like a rocket, then swerves away, out of control. "What can I do?" gasps the little bear, twisting the steering-wheel. "It's heading for that tree! There's going to be a crash!"

Rupert's efforts are all in vain, and he can only shut his eyes and wait for the crash. Next instant there is a tremendous bump, and the little bear is lifted right out of his seat, still hanging on to the steering-wheel but quite unharmed. "Whew!" he gasps. "How lucky that the inventor padded these trees!" But now everything seems to turn upside down as the car cannons into the trees one after another, until Rupert is dizzy and shaken. "Oh, this is awful," he moans.

RUPERT PLEASES THE IMPS

But Rupert gets control at last,
Although, he's speeding just as fast.

He pulls up, as an Imp leaps on,
"Well, did you catch it? Where's it gone?"

His news delights those Imps indeed,
And once more Rupert drives at speed.

He answers Algy with a frown,
"Hi, there! Sorry I can't slow down!"

Rupert struggles with the steering-wheel, wrenching it about until at last he begins to get the car under control. It still zig-zags alarmingly, but after a while the boffit becomes calmer, and to Rupert's relief he can steer his way along without bumping into things. Presently he spies a small figure waiting by a tree, and manages to pull up alongside. The first-aid Imp of Spring leaps on to the bumper car. "Did you catch the thing?" he shouts above the noise of the engine. "Is there any danger now?" The Imp is overjoyed to learn that the boffit has been trapped, and after thanking Rupert he runs to tell his friends that all their troubles are over. Rupert is anxious to return to the inventor so he presses the starter, and with a sudden jerk the car zooms on its way. "Hi, Rupert!" an astonished voice comes from behind a tree. It is Algy Pug, who has been searching for his pal. "Sorry I can't slow down!" cries the little bear. "This car is hard to manage!"

RUPERT DESERVES A REWARD

"Good!" the Inventor beams. "Well done!
It's safe now, and you've earned some fun!"

"Here's a reward your chums can share,
Four funfair tickets, little bear!"

The chums race homeward through the dell,
"Podgy and Bill can come as well!"

"I'd come if I weren't quite so old!"
Smiles Gaffer, when their tale is told.

Rupert pulls up outside the strange house, and a little later Algy comes puffing along to join him. The inventor is delighted at Rupert's success. "Well done!" he cries. Then he opens the car front, removes the boffit and squeezes its powerful springs until they are locked. "It's quite safe now," he chuckles. While Algy is admiring the car, the inventor beckons Rupert aside and hands him some funfair tickets. "There's your reward, little bear," he says. "Now you can go on the proper bumper cars." After thanking the kindly inventor, the two chums set off. "We've enough tickets for Bill and Podgy too!" says Rupert. "What fun it will be!" In the village the chums meet old Gaffer Jarge and Rupert stops to explain about the boffit and to show the tickets. "Oi, didn't you get a ticket for me?" frowns the Gaffer, pretending to be disappointed. Then he chuckles, "If I were a bit younger I'd go on those bumper cars myself!" he declares. "Aren't you lucky!"

RUPERT ENJOYS THE FUNFAIR

Says Mummy, when she's heard it too,
"That's just the right reward for you!"

The pals take Podgy Pig and Bill
Off to the funfair, with a thrill.

They wander past the roundabouts,
"Follow those loud bumps!" Rupert shouts.

"Oo, this is splendid!" laugh the chums,
Swish—BUMP! "Look out! Here Rupert comes!"

The chums say goodbye to Gaffer Jarge and hurry on to find Mrs Bear at the gate. "Just look!" they exclaim, gaily waving the tickets. Mrs Bear listens in astonishment to Rupert's story. "Well I never," she says. "I can see you're going to enjoy the rest of the day!" The happy pair run off to collect Bill Badger and Podgy Pig, and the four chums race to the funfair. "Come on," laughs Rupert. "Let's try the bumper cars first!" Soon they are in the midst of the funfair, and as they wander past the amusements Rupert pauses, listening intently. "I've heard those bumps before!" he exclaims. "This way, everybody!" Sure enough, the chums find the bumper cars just beyond the roundabouts, and in no time they are whizzing to and fro in the little cars, bumping into each other as they go. "Isn't this wonderful, Algy!" shouts Rupert above the din. "And much easier than driving the inventor's car, I can tell you! Especially after I'd caught the boffit!"

RUPERT and

It's here at last, the holiday!
And Rupert's come to Shrimpsea Bay!

Shrimpsea Bay! The holiday has really begun! Rupert with his Mummy and Daddy makes his way along the sea-front towards their holiday house. "I'll run ahead and find it!" he laughs. "What is it called?" His Mummy smiles: "'San Remo', like the place in Italy." So Rupert dashes on ahead and soon spies 'San Remo'. "Here it is!" he shouts, pointing with his stick of Shrimpsea rock at a pleasant-looking house.

he OCEAN OFFICE

"Ah, there's the house name, large and clear.
Mummy, Daddy, come on! We're here!"

"Why, Bill! You're here, too! And what's more,
We shall be living right next door!"

Then—"Rupert"—a familiar voice rings out, and he turns to find his best pal, Bill Badger. "Bill!" he exclaims. "What ... ?" Bill chuckles at his amazement and says: "We changed our minds about going to Greyrocks Cove and came here instead. I'm on my way to book a rowing boat for tomorrow. Can you come with me?" Rupert's Mummy who has just come up says that he may, but that the pals mustn't be too long. So off they run.

"Yes, you may go onto the beach,
But don't stray too far out of reach."

RUPERT AND BILL BOOK A BOAT

"Come on, let's fix up for a row!"
Says Bill, and to the shore they go.

"Whatever are you going to do?"
"Why, fold this little boat in two."

"These boats can't sink! You'll hire one? When?"
Smiles Bill, "Tomorrow morning, then."

Bill laughs. "I'm glad those boats can't sink.
We'll have a super trip, I think."

Rupert and Bill scurry along the sand to where the cliffs begin. "There's where the rowboats are kept!" says Bill pointing to a shed near the edge of the sea. "The man's there. Let's go and fix up a row for tomorrow." As they get near the shed they see that the man is pulling an odd sort of boat out of the water. "Can I do anything for 'ee?" he asks cheerily. But for a moment the two pals are speechless as they watch the man undo some bolts in the middle of the boat then fold the little craft in two. "Never seen a folding boat afore, eh?" chuckles the man. "Mine are all like that. Makes 'em easy to store." "Are they safe?" asks Rupert. "'Course they are!" the man replies. "You just can't sink 'em!" The chums look at each other. "Shall we try one?" Rupert asks. "Yes, let's!" says Bill. So the pals tell the man that they will hire one of his boats next day. Then they hurry back to the sea-front where Mrs Bear is watching for them from "San Remo".

RUPERT EXPLAINS THE BOAT

"Look!"—Rupert cuts his bread—"Here's how
That rowboat folded up just now."

Smiles Mrs Bear, "It's time for bed.
You'll be up early, sleepyhead."

"Oh, Bill!" cries Rupert. "This is fine!
Your bedroom's right next door to mine!"

When Rupert wakes the sun is bright.
He bounds from bed with great delight.

At supper Rupert tells his Mummy and Daddy about the odd sort of boat Bill and he plan to take out next day. They look startled when he says that it folds up. But Rupert laughs and tells them how the boat folds, showing them with two pieces of bread. "I say, that *is* a clever idea," agrees Mr Bear. Later when he is going to bed Rupert asks about something that has been puzzling him. "Why is this house called 'San Remo'?" he asks. "It's an odd sort of name." "Perhaps the owners think it sounds rather nice," Mummy suggests. When Mrs Bear has gone downstairs Rupert gets up to have one more glimpse of the sea. To his delight he finds that Bill has a room like his in the house next door. "Isn't it nice being neighbours?" Bill laughs. "Well, see you in the morning!" And so the pals go off to sleep at the end of their first day at Shrimpsea. Next day the sun is streaming in when Rupert wakens. He leaps out of bed and bangs on the wall to let Bill know he's up.

RUPERT AND BILL SET TO SEA

*"I've broken up some rock for you.
There's plenty for your friend Bill, too."*

*"Remember, if you lose your way,
You're from 'San Remo' you must say."*

*"Good morning to 'ee and your pal.
And here's your boat, the 'Shrimpsea Sal'."*

*"Keep in the bay for safety's sake.
Crag rock's the furthest you should make."*

Anxious to get off on his boat trip with Bill, Rupert hurries through breakfast. But before he leaves "San Remo" his Daddy gives him a few words of advice about being careful in a boat and his Mummy hands him a paper bag. "I've broken up that stick of rock for you," she says. "Thank you, Mummy," says Rupert, peering into the bag. "Oo! Every piece has 'Shrimpsea Bay' on it!" Then he stuffs the bag in his pocket and hurries off to find Bill. "If you get lost and have to ask the way home, remember you're from 'San Remo'," Mrs Bear calls after him. The pals reach the boat shed just as the man unfolds one of the little craft and launches it. "'Morning!" he calls to the chums. "Here's your boat—just your size—the 'Shrimpsea Sal'." Rupert sees that the name is painted on the side. Then Bill fetches the oars and the man pushes out the boat. "Don't go beyond your rock called the Crag," he says pointing out to sea. "The current's strong further out."

RUPERT ROWS TO THE CRAG

*The boat is launched and off they go
With Rupert as the first to row.*

*"You've made it," Bill says with a smile.
"Let's go ashore and rest a while."*

*Bill takes the rock and smiles, "I say,
Each piece of it reads 'Shrimpsea Bay'!"*

*Bill glances out to sea. "Oh, my!
I don't like that dark stormy sky."*

Rupert takes his first turn at rowing. He is a bit clumsy at first but he soon gets used to the feel of the oars and settles down to row steadily. "I must say you're doing well," says Bill. "You've not muffed a single stroke yet." All the time he is pulling towards the rock called the Crag Rupert is remembering what the boatman said about not going beyond it. When at last the boat comes to a gentle stop against the rock Rupert lets out a great sigh: "Whew! My arms are beginning to ache a bit." "Then let's get out and rest for a while and I'll do the rowing when we go back," Bill says. As the pals clamber onto the Crag, Rupert exclaims, "I'm starving. It must be the rowing." Then he remembers the bag of rock in his pocket and pulls it out. "Have a bit, Bill," he offers. "Oo, thanks," says his pal. "I say, every piece has 'Shrimpsea Bay' on it." When they've eaten enough Rupert puts the rest back in his pocket. "Those clouds look stormy," says Bill suddenly.

RUPERT SPIES A GIANT WAVE

"Let's get back quick! The sea's turned rough!
A storm is brewing, sure enough."

Cries Rupert, "Bill, it seems to me
We're being carried out to sea!"

Bill gasps, "I can't row any more."
Just then there comes a frightening roar!

Then with a terrifying sound,
Wild water surges all around!

Rupert doesn't like the look of the darkening sky either. "There's a storm coming, I'm sure," he says. "Come on, Bill. Let's get back at once!" The chums waste no time and soon Bill is pulling strongly towards the land. But all the time the sea is growing rougher. "We're not making much headway in this swell," pants Bill as he struggles to keep his oars in the water. Rupert who has his face towards the land suddenly exclaims in alarm: "We're not getting any nearer the shore! Oh, Bill, we're being carried out to sea!" Bill turns to look at the disappearing land then starts rowing harder than ever. But the little boat is driven further and further out to sea. At last Bill can row no more and droops across the oars. Rupert is just about to take the oars and try when he utters a cry of dismay. A giant crested wave is bearing down on their little craft. Rupert just has time to shout, "Hold tight, Bill!" before the wave is upon them, lifting the boat up and up and up!

RUPERT FINDS HIMSELF ALONE

The water spout's a frightening sight.
Grimly the two chums hang on tight.

When down once more his boat is thrown,
Poor Rupert finds that he's alone!

Though both are safe, the currents start
To pull the two half-boats apart!

As Rupert groans, "What shall I do?"
A tropic isle comes into view.

Desperately the chums cling to their tiny boat as it is swept along at great speed on top of the towering wave. Suddenly the wave begins to sink and Rupert shuts his eyes when he finds himself whirling dizzily downward. There is a bump that sends him sprawling. Then as quickly as it came the great wave is gone leaving Rupert breathless and shaken. "Bill, are you all right?" he calls. There is no answer. Rupert picks himself up and looks around. Bill's half of the boat is gone! Oh, no!

Rupert gazes wildly about. But wait! Surely that's it over there. And Bill still has the oars. What's more he has seen Rupert and is shouting, "I'm coming!" What a relief! Then in the same moment Rupert's hopes are dashed. The current is carrying him rapidly away from Bill! Bill's yells grow faint and soon Rupert is alone and dismally wondering if he will ever see home again. Then just when he has almost given up all hope an island comes into view.

RUPERT REACHES AN ISLAND

The boat glides on till Rupert lands
Upon the island's golden sands.

"I only hope that Bill's all right."
But Rupert's pal is not in sight.

"This is the Ocean Office, see?
King Neptune's! For Lost Property!"

"There is the walrus over there,
And he's in charge here, little bear."

To Rupert's joy he finds that the current which took him away from Bill is now carrying him to the island. Soon his half boat is bumping gently on a sandy beach. He jumps out and gazes round him. "Those are palm trees," he murmurs. "And there are so many strange flowers and bushes! Is it a tropical island, I wonder?" Then he remembers Bill and he climbs onto a nearby rock and gazes seaward. But there is not even a speck to be seen on the wide blue ocean.

Suddenly one of the seagulls which have been hovering over the beach swoops and speaks to the little bear. "I suppose you're lost, eh? I don't suppose you'd be here otherwise." Then, seeing Rupert's puzzled look, it adds sharply, "Didn't you know this is the Ocean Office, King Neptune's Lost Property Office?" Rupert shakes his head. "Then you'd better see the walrus!" the seagull squawks. "There he is among the palms." Looking, Rupert makes out a large figure.

RUPERT MEETS THE WALRUS

"Since he's in charge, the walrus may
Have me sent back to Shrimpsea Bay."

Some crabs come past with seaside toys
Lost on the beach by girls and boys.

"Well done, hard-working octopus!
You've found the most lost things for us."

The walrus grunts, "What's this we've got?
Were you washed up or found or what?"

The seagull flies off leaving Rupert wondering what it meant about the "Ocean Office" and having to see the walrus. "I suppose the walrus must be in charge of the island," he thinks. "So perhaps I better go and speak to him." He is making his way rather nervously towards the distant figure among the palm trees when a large crab scuttles past him carrying a child's spade and a toy boat. It is followed by other crabs all carrying things in their claws. And they are heading straight for the walrus. Under cover of the bushes, Rupert gets his first good look at the walrus, wearing a uniform and seated at a desk. He sees the crabs hand over their articles to the walrus. They are followed by an octopus carrying several oddments. "Well done!" the walrus tells it. "You must be the hardest working of the sea folk!" When the octopus has gone Rupert steps forward. "Hello," says the walrus, looking up. "How did you arrive here? Were you found or washed up?"

RUPERT GIVES HIS ADDRESS

"Ah well, since you have drifted here,
That counts as 'Lost', young bear, I fear."

"You'd be surprised how much we find.
Look. Someone's left a pail behind."

"'Present From Limpet Sands', I learn.
That should be easy to return."

"No—I've no label!" Rupert stares.
"I'm from 'San Remo'," he declares.

Rupert is taken aback by the walrus's question. "Oh, p-please," he stammers, "I drifted here in a boat, or rather half a boat." "Drifted, eh? Then you're lost," grunts the strange creature. "Well, you've certainly come to the right place. This is King Neptune's Lost Property Office. We collect all the things that are lost in the sea. Now I'd like a few particulars ... " Just then up comes a crab with a seaside pail. "What a busy day this is," says the walrus. "Excuse me while I attend to this."

He takes the pail and examines it all over. "'A Present From Limpet Sands'," he reads out. "Good! No trouble sending this back. Most of the stuff we get here has no clue about where it's come from ... by the way, do you have a label or something?" Quite bewildered by all that has been happening, Rupert stares back blankly. "I'm sorry, I haven't," he falters. Then he remembers what his Mummy told him before he left. "I-I'm from 'San Remo'," he blurts out.

RUPERT IS NOT UNDERSTOOD

"What's that? San Remo, did he say?
My goodness, that's a long, long way."

"San Remo? Let's see—here we are!
In Italy! You have come far!"

"So now we know where you must go."
"But it's not that San Remo—no!"

The weary walrus wipes his brow:
"Well, put him in 'UNCLAIMED' for now."

"He's from San Remo! What a distance to have come!" A gabble of astonished cries makes Rupert swing round. Facing him is a collection of odd-looking sea creatures who have been listening to him. Even the walrus seems startled at Rupert's words. "San Remo!" he repeats. "It is a long way off! Never known such a journey by a piece of lost property. Now, let's see … " He crosses to a globe of the world. "San Remo. In Italy if I'm not mistaken. Yes, here it is!" he exclaims. The walrus smiles in a satisfied sort of way. He is clearly pleased with himself. "Right, little bear, we'll soon get you home to Italy." "Italy!" gasps Rupert. "I don't want to go to Italy! I want 'San Remo' in Shrimpsea Bay where my Mummy and Daddy and I are staying!" The walrus passes a flipper wearily across his forehead. "Oh dear!" he sighs. "San Remo in Shrimpsea Bay! This piece of lost property is confused. Put it in UNCLAIMED for now."

RUPERT SPIES BILL'S BOAT

"'Lost Pets'," the crab says. *"Yes, that's you.*
Wait here till we think what to do."

"I wish that they'd pay heed to me ...
But, wait! There's something out to sea!"

"It's dear old Bill! He is all right!
Hello-o-!" shouts Rupert with delight.

A young sea-serpent, swift and strong,
Is pushing Bill's small boat along.

Next thing Rupert knows he is standing beside the dumps where all the lost property is stored. He has been taken there by one of the big crabs which grumbled all the way: "All this prattling about San Remo being Shrimpsea Bay. You are in a fine muddle. Better stay near the sign that says 'Lost Pets' until we decide how we're to get you home to Italy." Then it scuttled away before Rupert could repeat that he didn't want to go to Italy. Suddenly as he is standing there feeling miserable Rupert looks out to sea and notices a speck moving. Hardly daring to hope, he runs to a rock and climbs onto it for a better view. "Oh, yes!" he gasps. "It is Bill! But what's that pushing his boat?" Then as his pal's craft draws nearer he sees that it is being propelled by a young sea-serpent. "Hello-ooo there!" he shouts. "I'm here, Bill!" The little boat turns towards Rupert and across the water he hears Bill call, "I'll be right with you, Rupert!"

RUPERT'S PAL TRIES TO HELP

"Oh, Bill, I'm so glad that you've come!"
Cries Rupert as he greets his chum.

He sighs, "No matter what I say,
I can't prove I'm from Shrimpsea Bay."

"My boat can prove it! Look! Its name
Makes plain from Shrimpsea Bay we came!"

"I'll find the walrus and explain,"
Says Bill. "I'll soon be back again."

As Bill's boat nears the shore Rupert runs down to the water's edge to meet him. "Oh, Bill, how glad I am to see you!" he cries as his pal jumps ashore and clasps his hands. "And I'm glad to see you!" he laughs. "When we drifted apart I was afraid we'd lost each other for ever. I rowed and rowed without getting anywhere at all. Luckily I was spotted by this young sea-serpent which has pushed me all the way to the island. But I never dreamed I'd find you waiting here. And what sort of place is this?" Excitedly Rupert tells Bill all that has happened to him and about how the walrus wants to send him to Italy. "They don't seem to want to understand," he winds up. "If I only had something to prove I'm from Shrimpsea Bay!" Bill frowns. "That's awkward," he muses. "But wait! I can prove we're from Shrimpsea Bay. The name's on my part of the boat!" With rising hopes Rupert tells him where to find the walrus and Bill marches off to put matters right.

RUPERT IS TOLD HE MUST GO

Now Bill returns with gloomy face:
"He's sure you're from that other place."

"San Remo, Italy, he said.
He means to send you there instead!"

"The walrus wouldn't let me tell
Your ... " CLANG! The crab has rung a bell.

In answer to the bell's command
Sea-horses swim towards the land.

A little later, just after the young sea-serpent has said goodbye and swum back out to sea, Rupert spies Bill returning. His heart sinks for he can see that his chum looks gloomy. "Well, is it all right, Bill?" he asks anxiously. Bill heaves a sigh: "No, it isn't, Rupert. I explained how we were separated. But that walrus didn't even want to understand. He just kept saying that you had told a different story. He's made up his mind you come from San Remo in Italy and that you must go back there!"

Rupert gasps in dismay and Bill nods glumly. "It's awful," he agrees. "I'm being sent to Shrimpsea Bay because I have proof that I come from there. But the walrus won't hear of your coming with me. No amount of explaining seemed to make any difference." "Oh dear," quavers Rupert. "What will Mummy and ... " But Rupert is cut short by the clanging of a bell which is being rung by a crab. Then the chums hear a swishing and turn to see three big sea-horses!

RUPERT AND BILL PART AGAIN

"Into your boat! No time to lose!
San Remo! No, you can't refuse!"

"Oh, please ... " But Rupert pleads in vain.
The crabs will not let him explain.

"To San Remo in Italy!
Tomorrow you'll be there for tea."

Wistfully Rupert calls, "Goodbye!
Tell Mummy where I've gone and why."

While Rupert and Bill are still wondering what is happening several more crabs appear, all waving their claws excitedly. "Come on, hurry!" urges a big bossy crab as it edges Rupert towards his tiny boat. "You're for San Remo, Italy! Into the boat and we'll harness up the sea-horses!" Meanwhile Bill is having to get his boat ready. In a last attempt to stay with his chum, Rupert pleads: "It really is an awful mistake! My home isn't in Italy! Please let me go back to Shrimpsea Bay!" But like all the other creatures of King Neptune's Lost Property Office the crab doesn't want to pay any attention to Rupert's pleas: "You'll travel first by sea-horse express, then porpoise overnight sleeper then by sea service to San Remo in Italy. You should be there by teatime tomorrow." In no time at all Rupert finds himself being towed out to sea. In despair he calls out to his chum, "G-goodbye, Bill! Please tell my Mummy and Daddy what's happened to me!"

RUPERT REMEMBERS SOMETHING

"Rupert," Bill cries, "goodbye for now!
Be sure we'll get you back somehow!"

The little bear's heart really sinks.
"Oh, what a fix I'm in," he thinks.

He starts up as they gather speed:
"I know the very thing I need!"

"Please take me back without delay!"
The sea-horses at once obey.

"Don't give up, Rupert!" Bill shouts. "We'll get you back somehow. I'll tell your Mummy and Daddy what's happened and … " Rupert strains to hear Bill's words as they grow fainter and he is towed away by the team of sea-horses. Faster and faster go the sea-horses while Rupert grows more and more miserable. "Oh dear what a fix I'm in," he sighs. "Goodness only knows when I shall see Mummy and Daddy at Shrimpsea Bay again." Then suddenly, when the island is just a blur on the horizon, Rupert remembers something that jolts him out of his gloom. "It's the very thing! I know it is!" he cries. "It *will* work! It simply has to!" With his hopes beginning to rise again, he shouts to the sea-horses which by this time are fairly racing through the water, "Oh, please, turn back. Take me back to the island!" For a moment Rupert thinks that they are going to ignore him, but then they turn in a wide sweep and with Rupert hanging on tightly head back to the island.

RUPERT RETURNS TO THE ISLAND

He frees the creatures from the boat
And leaves the little craft to float.

Then as he glides towards the shore,
He meets his startled pal once more.

"I may convince the walrus now!
My plan's worth trying anyhow."

Says Rupert, "I've some proof for you.
It shows that what I said was true.

As the willing sea-horses pull his boat back to the island, Rupert grows more and more certain that his plan will work. When they enter shallow water he unfastens the tow ropes and sets the sea-horses free. Smoothly his little craft glides to the shore where Bill's boat has been harnessed to another team of sea-horses in readiness for his trip back to Shrimpsea Bay. "Hi, Bill!" Rupert shouts. "Maybe I shan't have to go to Italy after all!" "What's all this?" gasps Bill, dumbfounded.

Rupert leaps ashore and at once is joined by his bewildered chum. "No time to tell you now!" gasps Rupert. "But I'm hoping everything is going to be all right. Come on!" And with Bill at his heels, he dashes to the walrus's Ocean Office. "What! You again!" exclaims the walrus when the little bear rushes up. "I thought we'd dealt with your case." Breathlessly, Rupert explains: "I've come back to show you something!" And from his pocket he takes the rest of his rock.

RUPERT SHOWS HIS ROCK

He shakes the rock lumps out: "That's it!
Look! 'Shrimpsea Bay' on every bit!"

"H'm, where's my magnifying glass?
Yes—'Shrimpsea Bay'—this proof will pass."

"He knows we're both from Shrimpsea Bay
At last!" laughs Bill. "Let's get away!"

The crab says, "If you're being sent
To Shrimpsea Bay, it's time you went!"

Rupert shakes several lumps of his seaside rock onto the walrus's desk. "Please," he begs, "look at this. Surely this will prove I've come from Shrimpsea Bay!" Bill has arrived by now and he and Rupert hold their breath while, very slowly, the walrus examines the rock through a magnifying glass. After a pause he waggles his whiskers and says, "Yes, I can see the words 'Shrimpsea Bay' quite clearly. It's safe to say you've come from there. It's as good as a label. Why didn't you show me before?" "Because I didn't think of it!" cries Rupert. At once the walrus gives a fresh set of orders to his sea folk for both pals to be taken to Shrimpsea Bay. Rupert and Bill hurry to the shore where Bill bolts the two parts of their boat together again. While he is doing this one of the crabs calls Rupert's attention by snapping its claws. "I hear you're being sent to Shrimpsea Bay now," it says. "Yes, I'm going with my chum," laughs Rupert. "Isn't it wonderful!"

RUPERT AND BILL SPEED HOME

The three sea-horses start to pull,
The chums laugh, "This is wonderful!"

"A funny crowd, those Neptune's folk."
"Yes," Bill agrees. "But not a joke."

Cries Rupert, "We're going really fast!
For those were flying fish we passed."

The three slow down in sight of land.
"Now we can row, they understand."

As soon as Bill has fastened the two parts of the boat together securely he shouts to Rupert, "Come on! Aren't you ready to go?" Rupert dashes across to the boat and scrambles aboard, laughing, "Of course, I'm ready, Bill! You don't think I want to stay here any longer, do you?" Then Bill calls to their team of sea-horses and slowly the boat is pulled away from the shore. A group of the sea folk have gathered on the shore to watch the chums go, and as Rupert waves to them he says, "What an odd crowd they are. I don't think that I liked being one of their bits of lost property." Now, as the island disappears the little boat is hauled along at great speed. It even overtakes a school of flying fish. Then at last land comes into view and the sea-horses slow down until the boat comes to a stop. "I think we're there," says Bill. "Yes, this is as far as they'll take us," Rupert agrees. "They know we can row the rest." And he turns the sea-horses loose.

RUPERT'S DADDY IS WAITING

A worried Mr Bear looks out.
"They're here!" he gives a joyful shout.

The boatman greets them, "My, we're glad
To see you! That there storm was bad!"

"Wait till you hear what we have seen!
And guess where I have nearly been!"

"Now, home! And I'll tell on the way
How Shrimpsea Bay rock saved the day!"

On shore a very worried Mr Bear is scanning the sea with a pair of powerful glasses. Suddenly, to his great relief, he catches sight of the distant rowboat. "I can see them!" he exclaims. "Yes, I can see both Rupert and Bill!" "That's summat to be thankful for," says the old boatman standing at his side. "I was afeared we might never see them again after that storm." He wades into the water as the boat draws near. "It's good to see you!" he cries. "You had us all mighty anxious!"

As the kindly boatman pulls the boat up onto the slipway, Rupert who is first ashore, runs to his Daddy and throws himself into his arms. "Oh, it's lovely to be back!" he cries. "We've been such a long way! And so much has happened!" Daddy hugs the little bear and swings him off his feet. "I'm sure it has!" he says. "But now you're both safe and sound and you can tell us all about it later." Then Mr Bear and Rupert and Bill say goodbye to the boatman and go laughing home.

RUPERT
and the
Nut Hatch

John Harrold.

RUPERT AND BILL LOOK FOR CONKERS

This autumn Bill and Rupert plan
To find some conkers, if they can ...

"That's very strange! There's nothing here –
It's where we find them every year ..."

As Rupert searches, Bill sees two
More Nutwood chums come into view.

"Hello!" calls Algy. "All we've found
Are just these, lying on the ground."

It is autumn in Nutwood. The leaves of the trees have started to turn and Rupert and Bill are up on the common, looking for conkers ... "Have you found any yet?" asks Bill. "None!" says Rupert. "All I can see are leaves ... " "Me too!" nods his pal. "I suppose somebody must have beaten us to it!" "Probably Freddy and Ferdy!" laughs Rupert. "I expect they came out early and gathered all they could find. Even so, it does seem odd. I can't even see any empty husks ... "

Rupert and Bill try looking under all their favourite trees but they can't find a single conker. They are still searching when Bill spots two familiar figures, strolling across the common ... "Hello!" calls Algy Pug. "Looking for conkers? You'll be lucky to find any up here! Willie and I have tried everywhere we can think of and all we've found are these!" "Two!" blinks Rupert. "There are normally plenty for everyone. I wonder why they're suddenly so difficult to find?"

RUPERT HEARS SOMETHING'S WRONG

The pals are both surprised to see
Old Gaffer Jarge beneath a tree ...

"Sweet chestnuts are my favourite kind –
But it seems there are none to find!"

The chums try every tree they know –
But still don't have a thing to show ...

"The squirrels were complaining too –
They've had a fruitless search, like you!"

Deciding to continue with their search, Rupert and Bill are surprised to come across Gaffer Jarge ... "I didn't know you played conkers!" smiles Rupert. "Conkers?" scoffs the old man. "'Taint conkers I'm after! They're horse chestnuts. Sweet chestnuts are what I want. For roasting on the fire. Delicious, they are! Different husks to conkers. More prickles. Pale green. I'd show you one, if I could. Haven't found any all morning! I can't think what's happened to them all ... "

Leaving Gaffer Jarge to look for sweet chestnuts, Rupert and Bill continue on their way but still don't have any luck ... "I don't believe it!" sighs Bill. "We haven't found a single conker!" "You're not the only ones to complain," calls a nearby voice. "Horace!" blinks Rupert. "Shouldn't you be hibernating by now?" "Nearly time!" smiles the hedgehog. "As soon as the weather turns cold. The squirrels have been searching too, you know! Acorns, beech-nuts, they're all in short supply!"

RUPERT INVESTIGATES

"I've never known nuts disappear
Like this in any other year!"

A squirrel scampers down to tell
How she's heard something odd as well ...

She bounds ahead from tree to tree –
"I'll lead the way! Just follow me!"

"That's it!" she cries. The chums can hear
A droning sound from somewhere near ...

"It's strange!" yawns Horace. "I've never known conkers disappear like this! Squirrels hoard acorns, but they wouldn't take horse chestnuts." "Certainly not!" calls a voice. "They taste horrible!" Looking up, the pals see a squirrel peering from a nearby branch. "Horace!" she cries. "I heard a strange noise in the forest! It might be the creature that's taking all the nuts ..." "I'm afraid I'm too sleepy to be much help," says the hedgehog. "Why don't you show these two what you've found ... "

Leaping from tree to tree, the squirrel leads Rupert and Bill into the forest ... "It's kind of you to help!" she says. "We woodland creatures need a store of acorns and beech-nuts to survive the winter! If they keep disappearing like this there won't be enough to go round." As they follow their guide, the chums suddenly hear a strange droning sound. "That's it!" gasps the squirrel. "It certainly sounds strange," blinks Rupert. "Like ... like someone using a vacuum cleaner!"

RUPERT SPOTS SOME ELVES

The two chums can't believe their eyes –
"It's Autumn Elves! What a surprise!"

They gather conkers from the ground,
Collecting every one they've found ...

Rupert and Bill keep out of view,
Watching to see what the Elves do.

The chums are both surprised to see
A hatch cut in a hollow tree ...

As the chums creep forward, they are amazed to see two of Nutwood's Autumn Elves ... "They are using some sort of vacuum cleaner!" blinks Bill. "Sucking up the conkers!" gasps Rupert. "No wonder we couldn't find any ... " The pair stand staring in astonishment as each Elf fills the basket on his back with fallen chestnuts. "Husks and all!" whispers Bill. "What do you suppose they're up to? Why are the Elves hoovering up conkers? I thought they gathered nuts and seeds by hand ... "

Remembering how Nutwood's Elves like to go about their work secretly, Rupert and Bill keep out of sight as the pair walk off with their baskets full to the brim ... "What now?" whispers Bill. "They've stopped by an old oak ... " As the chums look on, they see the Elves open a hidden door. "It's hollow!" says Rupert. "Perhaps they're going to climb inside?" To his surprise, the Elves remove their baskets and tip them out in a cascade of husks and shiny conkers. "How odd!" he murmurs.

RUPERT SLIDES DOWN A CHUTE

The Elves empty their baskets then
Close up the secret hatch again ...

The pals approach the secret store.
"Let's try to open up the door!"

The hatch swings open, "What's inside?"
"A chute! It's like a metal slide ... "

As Bill leans forward, suddenly,
The pals fall down, into the tree!

As soon as the Elves have emptied their baskets, they shut the hatch and head off across the common towards another stand of trees ... "What do you make of that?" asks Bill. "It must be some sort of secret store!" "I wonder?" says Rupert. "The door looked easy enough to open. I don't suppose they'd mind if we took a peek ... " "Go on!" urges Bill. "Just a check, to see how many they've got. If all the Elves have been out gathering there won't be a conker left in the whole of Nutwood."

Pulling open the hatch in the hollow tree, Rupert finds a smooth metal chute which juts over a deep, dark pit ... "Gosh!" blinks Bill. "It's bigger than I thought! I wonder how far down it goes?" As his chum leans forward for a better view, Rupert suddenly feels the chute move, sending him sprawling into the darkness. "Help!" cries Bill. "The door's closing behind us!" Before he can stop, he finds himself sliding down after Rupert, towards the base of the hollow tree ...

RUPERT MEETS THE CHIEF ELF

The pair end up deep underground,
Where startled Elves are gathered round ...

The Elves crowd round and all begin
To ask the pals how they got in.

Their Chief appears. "What's this? Who's there?"
He calls out as he spots the pair.

"No harm done!" smiles the Chief. "Now you're
Down here, I'll take you on a tour ... "

As they go sliding down the chute, Rupert and Bill expect to reach the bottom almost immediately. Instead, they find themselves falling down a long, dark tunnel, which seems to go deep underground ... To their utter amazement, they finally emerge to a glow of bright lights, landing in a huge tub of conkers, which are being sorted by three more Autumn Elves ... "What? Who? How?" stammers their leader, looking even more startled than the Nutwood chums ...

"I'm sorry!" says Rupert. "We just couldn't resist looking inside the hollow tree ... " "You opened our hatch?" scowls one of the sorters. "Only Elves are allowed to do that! Not Nutwooders, like you ... " "Nutwooders?" calls a stern voice. "What are they doing here?" The Chief Elf demands to hear Rupert's story ... "Highly irregular!" he tuts. "But I can't really blame you for being curious ... " To the pals' delight, the Chief breaks into a broad smile. "Now you're here, I'll show you what happens next!"

RUPERT IS GIVEN A GUIDED TOUR

"Down here we sort the nuts we find –
Sweet chestnuts, conkers, every kind ... "

The pals are taken to be shown
How all the seeds and nuts are grown.

"Each conker that we plant has got
Some growing mixture in its pot ... "

"The little seedlings soon come out –
Bright light and tonic helps them sprout."

Forgiven by the Elves, Rupert and Bill find themselves being given a conducted tour by the Chief ... "You've seen how the nuts are gathered," he says. "And here you see them being sorted. Conkers in one box, sweet chestnuts in another. Beech nuts, acorns, they all need sorting out, you know. When the boxes are full we take them through to the Arboretum." "Arboretum?" blinks Rupert. "Tree nursery," smiles the Chief. "This is just the beginning. Growing trees is a lengthy business ... "

From the sorting chamber, Rupert and Bill are taken to another room, where Elves are busy planting conkers and acorns in individual flowerpots ... "Amazing!" blinks Rupert. "I wonder if I could grow a tree like that?" "Of course!" says the Elf. "You'd have to wait a bit longer than us, though. We use special growing mixture to speed things up a bit ... " "It's just like a factory!" gasps Bill. "What happens next?" "Seedlings!" says the Elf. "They're next door ... "

RUPERT SEES THE ARBORETUM

"These saplings look like little trees –
An oak will grow from each of these!"

"This way!" the Chief calls. "Follow me!
There's one more stage for you to see … "

"The trees spend one year here, then they
Are moved again, to where they'll stay."

"Our Arboretum lets us grow
New trees where we think they should go … "

"This way!" calls the Chief Elf. "These pots are full of seedlings. We grow them under extra bright lights and water them with tree tonic. You can see for yourselves how quickly they turn into little saplings … " "They're miniature trees now!" laughs Bill. "Oaks by the look of it." "That's right!" nods the Chief. "You can always tell by the shape of the leaves. I always make a final inspection, just in case any have been muddled up. These are nearly ready to be transferred outside … "

Following the Chief Elf, the chums reach a small, circular door … "We're back on the common!" Bill blinks. "The edge of it," nods the Chief. "This is where we harden off new trees. A season here in the open air and they're ready to be moved to their final homes … " "Remarkable!" says Rupert. "I thought new trees just grew wherever acorns or conkers fell to the earth … " "Forest management!" beams the Chief Elf. "This way we can control exactly what goes on … "

RUPERT PERSUADES THE CHIEF

"But what about the nuts and seeds
That every woodland creature needs?"

"You two were quite right to protest –
We'll stop now and leave all the rest!"

The Chief says he will make amends
And give some chestnuts to his friends ...

The Elves bring two big baskets out –
"Sweet chestnuts and conkers!" they shout.

"It sounds wonderful," says Rupert. "But what about all the woodland creatures? Your Elves have been so good at gathering nuts that there's none left for anyone else!" "Oh, dear!" sighs the Chief. "I suppose you're right! I never thought of anyone else ... " "Your Arboretum's still a good idea," says Rupert. "You just need to leave more behind ... " The Elf looks thoughtful, then breaks into a broad smile. "We will!" he cries. "We'll stop collecting nuts for this year and leave all the rest where they fall ... "

"Not only will we stop collecting," says the Chief Elf, "but our store of nuts will be used to make good any harm we've done!" "You mean you'll give some back?" blinks Bill. "Exactly!" nods the Chief. "Acorns for the squirrels and conkers for you! Perhaps you'd like some sweet chestnuts too?" "Yes, please!" laughs Rupert. "I know somebody in Nutwood who'd be very glad of those ... " In next to no time, two Elves appear with baskets filled to the brim. "One of each!" they smile.

RUPERT RETURNS WITH CHESTNUTS

"Goodbye!" the Elves call. "Next year we
Will leave nuts underneath each tree ... "

The chums show Gaffer Jarge their haul –
"We've got some chestnuts, after all!"

"Well done, you two! I'll roast the lot!
They taste delicious when they're hot ... "

"Hey! You two! Look what we've got here!
Enough conkers to last the year ... "

"Thanks for your warning!" calls the Chief Elf as the chums wave farewell. "Next year, we'll go back to gathering nuts by hand!" Walking back across the common, the pals spot Gaffer Jarge, still searching under a spreading tree ... "Come on!" laughs Rupert. "Let's show him what we've got!" "Hello, young 'uns!" says Gaffer Jarge. "What's that in those baskets?" "Chestnuts!" beams Rupert. "One's for you, while the other is for us to share ... "

"Chestnuts?" blinks the old man. "But I've been looking for those all morning ... " "We did have a bit of help," admits Bill. "Someone we met had been collecting too ... " "Good for them!" smiles Gaffer. "There's enough chestnuts here for the whole of Nutwood ..." Leaving Gaffer Jarge with his unexpected prize, Rupert and Bill go off in search of their chums, who are just as pleased to see their haul ... "Marvellous!" says Algy. "Now we can all play at conkers."

RUPERT'S HORSE HEAD PAPERFOLD

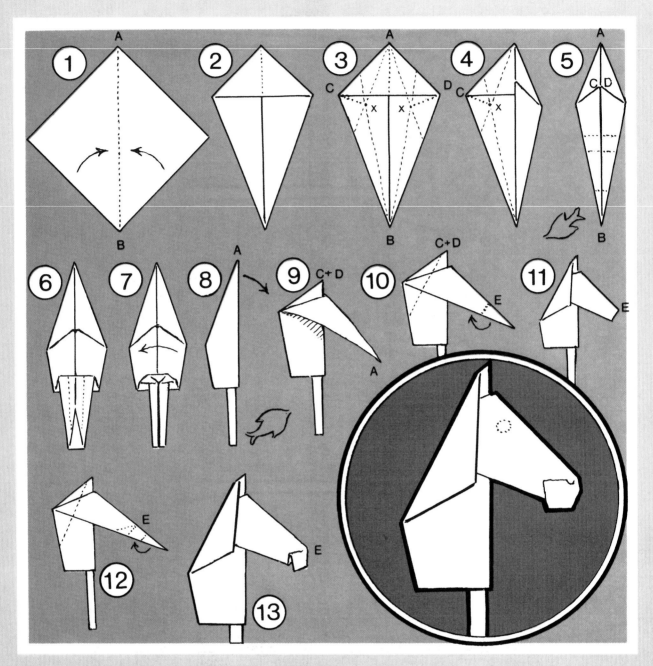

Going carefully, Rupert made this horse's head at the first attempt. (It was invented by a clever paperfolder, Martin Wall.) Take a square of thin paper. Fold it once as in Fig. 1, then fold both lower sides to the middle line (Fig. 2) and fold AC, BC, AD and BD in turn to the middle line to leave the pattern of creases in Fig. 3. Note the points marked X where the creases meet. Fold AD and BD together to the middle as far as you can and crease the line XD neatly (Fig. 4). Do the same with C (Fig. 5), making the points at C and D very sharp. To shorten the stem fold B up to A to form the top dotted line, bend B down again at the next line and fold the tip up to look like Fig. 6. Bend the lower sides inward by the new dotted lines and squash at the top to narrow the stem (Fig. 7). Fold the whole thing in half (Fig. 8). Pull A outward and turn it inside out (Fig. 9), revealing C and D which become the horse's ears. Decide on the length of head at E (Fig. 10) and reverse EA, pushing the tip under and out of sight. Bend down the left top corner for the mane and Fig. 11 is the simple horse's head. For a better nose return to Fig. 10, fold a smaller tip under and, using the two short dotted lines at E (Fig. 12), open the end and swivel it (Fig. 13) into the final position. If you mean to use it as a bookmark press it under something heavy. Draw the eyes rather high on the face.

RUPERT

and
Snowflake

Story devised and illustrated by Stuart Trotter.

RUPERT GOES CHRISTMAS SHOPPING

Young Rupert's mummy says that they
Must go Christmas shopping today.

Excited, Rupert wraps up warm,
In case there is a winter storm.

And Rupert can't believe his eyes.
Yes – snow is falling from the skies!

So Mr Bear drives carefully
While snowflakes fall more heavily.

It is the day before Christmas Eve, and Rupert has been playing happily indoors all morning. He is just deciding what to play next when Mrs Bear comes to speak to him. "We must drive into town to do some Christmas shopping," she says. "Oh, good," Rupert replies. "I want to see the Christmas lights!" Rupert tidies away his toys, Mrs Bear helps him put on his coat and soon Rupert, his mummy and his daddy are all wrapped up, ready for the shopping trip.

As they head out into the lane, snowflakes begin to drift down from the sky. Rupert is delighted and he jumps up and down, trying to catch them. "It looks like it will be a white Christmas in Nutwood this year!" he laughs happily. The Bears climb into the car and Mr Bear drives them all into town along the snowy lanes. Rupert gazes out of the window and watches happily as the snow begins to stick to the ground. Soon the whole road is covered in snowfall.

RUPERT SEES A STRANGE LITTLE TOY

The Town is quite a lovely sight,
The shops are lit with Christmas lights!

Now Rupert's asked if he'll assist
His mummy with the shopping list.

Whilst passing Mr Hound's toy shop
He sees a sight that makes him stop.

The moving toy now seems to hide
So Rupert quickly heads inside.

In the town centre all the buildings and shops are lit up with Christmas lights. It really is a lovely, festive sight, and Rupert can't wait to see the window displays. Mr Bear drops Rupert and Mrs Bear in the centre of town then drives off to park the car. "I need to pop to a shop round the corner," Mrs Bear says to Rupert. "We have quite a lot to get. Can you take this shopping bag and list and fetch these items for me?" "Of course, Mummy," Rupert smiles and sets off to find the items.

Rupert passes Mr Hound's toy shop and can't resist stopping to look at the Christmas display in the window. It is a wonderful display – Mr Hound has everything from cars to rocket ships. As he is admiring all the wonderful things in the display he sees a small, bluish-white toy that seems to be waving at him. Rupert blinks in amazement, and the toy disappears. Curious, Rupert heads inside to search for the strange little creature that seems to be alive.

RUPERT MEETS SNOWFLAKE

"However did you get back there?
And is this snow?" asks Rupert Bear.

"Oh, Mr Hound, how much is this?
I'd really love to purchase it."

"I cannot sell this toy, sadly.
This Snowflake's got a fault, you see."

"Well, never mind," says Rupert Bear,
And sets him on the shelf with care.

He finds the strange little toy sitting on a shelf right at the back of the shop and picks it up carefully. He is surprised that it feels cold to touch. And what's more, it is snowing inside the shop! Rupert examines the toy carefully. It isn't moving any more – but how did it get from the window to the back of the shop? There's something very odd about it, and no mistake. He picks it up and takes it to the counter. "Good morning, Mr Hound. How much is this toy?" Rupert asks.

"Oh, I'm afraid Snowflake isn't for sale," Mr Hound tells Rupert. "He's faulty, you see. Since he arrived, the oddest things keep happening – as you can see, it's snowing all over my shop. I put him on one shelf, and when I look again he's moved to another. It's very odd, I tell you! I'll be sending him back to Santa this week." Rupert is puzzled, but he thanks Mr Hound and puts Snowflake back on the shelf. Is Rupert imagining it, or is Snowflake's smile faltering?

RUPERT HAS A STOWAWAY

Unseen, Snowflake flies through the air,
He's heading straight for Rupert Bear!

As he leaves, Rupert doesn't see
His shopping bag has company.

At home, Mrs Bear asks, "What's this?
I'm sure this wasn't on the list!"

"That's strange, I will return him when
We next pop into town again."

Rupert wishes Mr Hound a very merry Christmas, picks up his shopping bag and with a cheery wave he heads for the door. Mr Hound turns to speak to another customer, so neither of them see what happens next. Snowflake has been watching Rupert, and is now creeping across the shelves towards him. Rupert is halfway out of the door when Snowflake leaps across the shop and lands silently in Rupert's bag. The mischievous toy is very much alive!

Back at home, Mrs Bear is unpacking the shopping when she finds Snowflake in Rupert's bag. "Whatever is this doing in here?" she asks. "I know this wasn't on the shopping list!" Rupert is astonished – he can't imagine how Snowflake got into the bag. He tells his mummy about visiting Mr Hound's shop and what Mr Hound said about Snowflake being an odd toy. "He must have fallen in," he tells Mrs Bear. "I'll take him back next time we go to town."

Says Rupert, "I shall put you here,
You're very sweet – I'll keep you near."

"I must say, I'm exhausted, so
Goodnight, and off to bed I'll go."

"But what's this?" gasps the little bear.
"However did you end up there?"

As dawn is breaking, Rupert wakes
To find his room filled with snowflakes!

As Rupert is getting ready for bed that evening he wonders what to do with Snowflake. He is rather a sweet thing and Rupert doesn't want to leave him squashed in the shopping bag. He looks for a safe place in his bedroom where Snowflake can sit for the night, and decides that the window ledge is the best place for him. Outside, the snow is still falling heavily. Rupert heads back into the living room to say goodnight to his parents, then returns to his room.

Rupert gasps. He knows he put Snowflake on the window ledge, but there he is, bold as brass, sitting on the bedpost! Now Rupert is sure he isn't imagining things; Snowflake is clearly a very mischievous toy indeed. Rupert sits Snowflake back on the window ledge, gets into bed and tries not to think about it any more as he goes to sleep. He wakes, shivering, as dawn is breaking. To his disbelief, it is snowing in his room. What's more, Snowflake is sat on his shoulder, poking him!

RUPERT LOSES SNOWFLAKE

Poor Rupert can't believe his eyes.
"Oh, Snowflake! You're alive!" he cries.

"Oh, wake up! Wake up!" Rupert cries.
"Why, what's wrong?" his daddy replies.

But Snowflake doesn't want to stay.
"Oh, goodness! He's getting away!"

"Oh, no!" says Rupert with a frown.
"I really have to track him down!"

Rupert sits bolt upright and the mischievous toy begins bouncing up and down on his bed. "You're alive!" Rupert splutters. "I knew it!" He dashes into his parents' bedroom – it is snowing in there, too. "Wake up!" he cries. "Snowflake is alive, and he's making it snow all over the house!" Mrs Bear groans and rolls over. "Eh? What?" Mr Bear mumbles sleepily. He sits up and his eyes widen as he sees that his bedroom is covered in snow. He is quite speechless.

Snowflake scurries into the room. Rupert makes a grab for him but he springs out of reach then jumps out of the window and away into the garden. "Oh, goodness!" Rupert gasps. "He's getting away! Oh, please may I go after him?" he asks Mr Bear, as Mrs Bear goes to fetch the dustpan and brush. "I can't lose him. He must go back to Mr Hound so he can be sent back to Santa!" "Yes, you had better find him," Mrs Bear says. "Just make sure you wrap up warm."

RUPERT SEES WILLIE MOUSE

Small footprints in the fallen snow
Show Rupert where he needs to go.

To Willie Mouse he gives a shout,
"Hi there! Why do you dance about?"

"Oh, Rupert! Help me catch this thing.
It's jumping around like a spring!"

But Snowflake, who was once quite small,
Is now a rather large snowball!

Rupert dresses quickly and leaves the house. Fortunately, Snowflake has left footprints in the fallen snow, so Rupert can easily follow him. The footprints lead up the lane and into the fields, and Rupert hasn't gone far when he spots his pal Willie Mouse who is building a snowman. He also seems to be dancing about in the snow, which is very odd. "Hi, Willie!" Rupert calls as he approaches. "Whatever are you doing? Why are you dancing about like that?"

As Rupert gets closer he realises Willie isn't dancing – he is jumping up and down. "I'm trying to catch this strange little thing, but it won't stay still. It's jumping about like a spring!" Willie replies breathlessly. "That's Snowflake," Rupert tells him. "I must get him back to Mr Hound's toy shop so that he can be sent back to Santa." At those words, Snowflake knocks the snowman's head clean off and begins to roll downhill with it through the snow, creating a rather large snowball.

RUPERT CHASES AFTER SNOWFLAKE

Right down the hill he rolls until
He reaches a complete standstill.

"Now Snowflake, we must make our way
To Mr Hound's without delay."

And for the second time today,
That pesky Snowflake runs away.

Young Rupert watches in alarm.
Will Snowflake come to any harm?

Rupert rushes after the snowball that has engulfed Snowflake, and finds it at the bottom of the hill. He quickly digs Snowflake out; the little toy looks flustered but seems unharmed. "Are you all right?" Rupert puffs. Snowflake smiles at Rupert and nods his head as he gets to his feet. "You really are quite mischievous, you know. Now then, I must get you back to Mr Hound's toy shop right away, so he can send you back to Santa," Rupert says. "Follow me, and I'll lead the way."

Snowflake's face falls. Rupert can see that he doesn't want to go back to the toy shop. Looking rather unhappy, Snowflake dashes off. "Bother!" Rupert exclaims. "Why must he keep dashing off?" He chases after Snowflake as quickly as he can. Ahead is a cliff face, and Rupert stops in his tracks as he sees Snowflake stumble towards the edge. A moment later, Snowflake disappears over the snowy cliff, tumbling towards the ground below. It is a very long drop and Rupert is alarmed.

RUPERT SEES A PLANE

Where there was one Snowflake before
Now there are many, many more!

Up in the sky a plane appears.
"The Little Cowboy!" Rupert cheers.

"I'm here for Snowflake," he explains.
"I've come to take him home again."

The Snowflakes jump and bounce around.
The pair search till each one is found.

As Snowflake hits the ground, Rupert is amazed to see him shatter into lots of tiny Snowflake toys. Rupert clambers down to see if the Snowflakes are all right, and is relieved to see that they are unhurt and bouncing around happily. Rupert smiles, but then his face falls: it was difficult enough chasing after one Snowflake, so how on earth will he get several Snowflakes back to the toy shop? As he is pondering this, a plane appears in the sky above. It's Rupert's friend, Santa's Little Cowboy!

The Little Cowboy lands his plane in the field next to the little bear. "Hi, Rupert!" he calls as he climbs out. "Santa sent me to come and collect that mischievous Snowflake as he heard from Mr Hound that he's faulty. But I see there are several of him now! Let's gather them all up and put them in my magic bag. The Toymaker isn't going to believe this!" Together they gather up all the bouncing Snowflakes and put them into the Little Cowboy's bag.

RUPERT FILES TO SANTA'S CASTLE

The magic bag begins to shake,
As if it is about to break!

The Cowboy can quite plainly see,
With Rupert Snowflake wants to be.

And so the three take off and fly
To Santa's castle in the sky.

The plane lands in the courtyard, where
The Toymaker is waiting there.

But as soon as the last Snowflake has been put in the bag, it begins to shudder and shake. Puzzled, the Little Cowboy peers inside and out jumps Snowflake into Rupert's arms, all in one piece again. "A magic bag indeed!" Rupert laughs. Snowflake hugs Rupert tightly and it's quite clear that he wants to stay with the little bear. "I hope you didn't have plans today, Rupert. It looks like you'll have to come with me to Santa's castle," the Cowboy chuckles.

Moments later, the three take off in the plane, flying north to Santa's castle. After a while the castle comes into sight – the clouds around it seem to be glowing with magic light. The Little Cowboy lands the plane in the courtyard where they are met by Santa's Toymaker. "Where is that mischievous Snowflake?" he asks. Rupert hands him over. "He's quite sweet, really," Rupert smiles. "Although he has led us on quite a merry chase today!"

RUPERT GOES TO THE TOYMAKER'S OFFICE

The Toymaker leads them away
To his office without delay.

He examines Snowflake in vain.
"I'm sorry, I just can't explain."

"Oho! Is this the fellow who
Has caused so much trouble for you?"

Because Snowflake's so wet and cold,
Poor Santa just can't keep his hold.

Clutching Snowflake carefully, the Toymaker leads Rupert and the Little Cowboy inside to his office which is full of old books and strange contraptions. The Toymaker sits down at his desk and examines Snowflake under his magnifying glass, looking for any clues as to why he is alive. He peers at the little toy for a long while, and Rupert and the Little Cowboy watch expectantly. Finally he looks up. "I'm sorry, I can't explain it," he sighs. "I don't know how this happened. It's a mystery."

Santa appears at the door. "Ah, Rupert!" Santa smiles, then sees Snowflake. "Oho! Is this the fellow who has caused so much trouble? Let me take a look at him." Santa picks up the mischievous toy. "I've seen this happen once before, and in that case, magic snowfall was to blame. I thought there was something odd about that snowstorm earlier … " But Snowflake suddenly slips out of Santa's hand. Rupert and the Cowboy know what's going to happen. "Not again," Rupert sighs.

RUPERT HELPS CATCH THE SNOWFLAKES

And as he hits the floor, he breaks
Into many bouncing Snowflakes.

"Quick! Come and help us catch them, and
Ask everyone to lend a hand!"

Says Santa, "We'll keep Snowflake here."
Delighted, Rupert gives a cheer.

The Little Cowboy starts his plane,
And flies young Rupert home again.

The mischievous toy breaks into many bouncing Snowflakes once more. They scatter across the floor and begin jumping all over Rupert, Santa and the Toymaker. The three try to catch them, but one by one the tiny Snowflakes bounce out of the Toymaker's office and into the courtyard. Santa, Rupert and the Toymaker dash out after them, calling for help as they go. "Quick! Help us catch them, and ask everyone you see to lend a hand!" Santa shouts to his workers.

Eventually, and with much effort from everyone, the Snowflakes are gathered up. "What will you do with him?" Rupert asks Santa. He feels rather sorry for Snowflake who obviously just wants to be loved. "He can live here, where I can keep an eye on him," Santa chuckles. The tiny Snowflakes smile too, and Rupert gives a cheer. "Well, I better be getting home. It is Christmas Eve, after all!" he smiles. Santa says goodbye, then the Little Cowboy starts up his plane and flies Rupert home.

RUPERT GETS A SPECIAL GIFT

His parents are still working hard
Shovelling snow into the yard.

"You won't believe the day I've had!"
Young Rupert tells his mum and dad.

Tomorrow is Christmas morning.
"I wonder what Santa will bring?"

And Rupert can't believe his eyes.
"My very own Snowflake!" he cries.

When Rupert finally gets home, he is amused to see that his parents are still hard at work, shovelling snow out of the house and into the yard. "Did you catch Snowflake?" Mrs Bear asks. "Yes, in the end," Rupert says, "but you won't believe what happened!" Mr Bear comes out of the house and they both listen to Rupert's story. "What a day you've had!" Mr Bear smiles. "Let's get you to bed. It's Christmas Eve, and I'm sure Santa will bring you something special tomorrow."

Rupert gets ready for bed and hangs his stocking on the bedpost. He is quite exhausted and quickly falls asleep. He wakes bright and early on Christmas morning and jumps out of bed to see what Santa has brought him. He opens his stocking and gasps. Inside is a small, familiar figure. There is a note attached, which says, "Happy Christmas Rupert, from Snowflake." "My very own Snowflake!" he cries happily. And this time, it really is just a toy.
Isn't it?